Tam O'Shanter

by

Lari Don

Illustrated by Peter Clover

4953155

In memory of Jim Mackay, who knew far more
about Burns than I ever will.
Lari Don

To Val and the loving memory of her father –
Peter Muckle Walls.
Peter Clover

First published in 2009 in Great Britain by
Barrington Stoke Ltd
18 Walker St, Edinburgh, EH3 7LP

www.barringtonstoke.co.uk

Copyright © 2009 Lari Don
Illustrations © Peter Clover

The moral right of the author has been asserted in
accordance with the Copyright, Designs and
Patents Act 1988

ISBN: 978-1-84299-784-0

Printed in Great Britain by Bell & Bain Ltd

Contents

Foreword

The story of Tam O'Shanter was made famous by the fact that it was written by the great Scottish poet Robbie Burns, who was born 250 years ago this year. The poem about Tam's night with the witches is known around the world – it was a great race for Tam to reach the bridge and safety before the witches could get to him.

As a dyslexic I have never, during all of my life, read all that many books, and when I do, I give them my total concentration and commitment and it's great that a book has been written about this famous experience of Tam O'Shanter, which came out of the mind of one of the greatest Scots the world has ever known.

I hope you enjoy the book, and we Scots would welcome you to Scotland, particularly in 2009, the year of our homecoming, but if not within that time-window, every year is a good year to come to Scotland.

Sir Jackie Stewart OBE
Formula One World Champion 1969, 1971, 1973

Chapter 1
Friday Night!

Nannie dropped her Granny's eyeballs on the kitchen floor. She was getting ready for her first Friday night dance, so she was feeling a bit nervous, and her fingers were shaking.

She picked the slippery eyes up, and put them in the front pocket of her dress. Her Granny had made this dress for her. It was a bit small now, but it was still her favourite. She wanted to look her best tonight. So she wiped her wet fingers on her dress, and started to brush her hair and sharpen her nails.

At the other end of the village, Tam O'Shanter was also getting ready for his Friday night out, counting coins into his wallet and brushing mud and straw off his best jacket. But Tam wasn't nervous. He went drinking with his friends in town every Friday night.

Tam rode his old grey horse Meg out of the farm-yard towards Ayr. It started to rain as Meg clattered across the old bridge over the River Doon, so he buttoned up his jacket.

Meg struggled up the steep hill from the river to the village of Alloway. Tam started to shiver as they passed Alloway's church. The church was so old it had no roof and the grave-stones scattered round were cracked and squint. He never liked passing this

church in the dark, because he had heard far too many spooky stories about the old kirk.

The rain got heavier as Tam and his horse splashed along the great road to Ayr. But Tam cheered up as they reached the town square. The sign above the pub was waving to him, flapping and squeaking in the gusting wind.

Friday night! Tam loved Friday night!

At last, Nannie was dressed up, ready to dance all night. But she had to take the long way round, because she couldn't go across the old Doon bridge. Nothing evil can cross running water, and surely only something evil carries her Granny's eyeballs in her pocket.

Chapter 2
Skint

Tam tipped his wallet upside down and shook it. No coins fell out. He patted his pockets, and checked under the table. No more coins. It was time to leave the pub. He pushed open the door, and the wind nearly blew him back into the arms of his singing friends. But they were leaving too, and with no money and no-one left to drink with, Tam really did have to go home, even though the storm had got much worse.

After a good Friday night, Tam sometimes didn't remember the way home on his own, but his horse always knew where her oats were. So when Tam climbed up onto her back, Meg started along her usual Friday night road home. The road which led out of the town, past the church at Alloway, over the old Doon bridge, then back to her stable.

Thunder bellowed loud, deep and long above Tam, and lightning struck tall tree-tops either side of him. The rattling rain was cold and hard. And Tam's old grey mare wouldn't go any faster than a slow walk through the dark and murky night.

Tam sat slumped in the saddle, and sang wee songs to himself, looking to both sides and behind him with every step Meg took, so that no ghosts could sneak up on him.

Tam and Meg passed the slope where a pedlar had frozen to death in the snow just last winter.

Could Tam still hear the pedlar's last chattering breaths? Were those his ribbons and needles scattered on the road? No! It was the wind in the trees, and the twigs blown onto the ground. But Tam sang even louder.

Meg stumbled past the tall trees and the big rock where Tam's mate Charlie had fallen and broken his neck a few summers past. Tam's hands held tight to Meg's reins and his legs held tight to her sides, so he wouldn't fall off.

Was that Charlie's hat? Caught on that branch? Was that Charlie's out of tune voice joining in with Tam's favourite drinking song? No! But Tam's voice shook as he sang the chorus.

Meg struggled through the mud past the old well where Mungo Scott's mother had drowned when Tam was a boy.

Was that a shiny wet hand reaching out from the water for help? Tam's heart beat faster and his breath grew tight in his throat. But Meg's plodding steps, slow and steady, taking him to the safety of home, calmed him down. There was no white hand. Tam shook his head. He had to stop seeing all these ghosts. They were just in his mind. There was nothing there, nothing hiding in the darkness. But now he was shouting the most cheerful songs he knew.

And Meg just kept on walking home.

Then suddenly, over the drums of the thunder, the howling of the wind and his own croaky voice, Tam heard a new music. Where was it coming from? He knew it couldn't be more ghosts on the road. The ghosts were just in his mind.

Then through the trees, Tam saw the church at Alloway. The church was rocking and shaking in time to fast music and wild laughing. And it was lit up like a bonfire. Bright cheerful light was streaming from every window, jabbing from every hole in the walls. The light, music and laughter were bubbling out of the top of the church like porridge boiling over from a small pot.

No matter what stories Tam had heard about the kirk at Alloway, he was always up for a party. And he had left the pub long before he was ready to go to bed. So he pulled Meg towards the church. This sounded like a party worth gate-crashing.

Meg took no notice of Tam, and kept walking home. He tugged on Meg's reins to steer her towards the church.

She stopped dead. And Tam's nose bumped into her wet hairy neck.

Annoyed now, Tam jabbed his feet into her old ribs, to urge the horse through the gate in the wall round the grave-yard. Meg walked even more slowly than usual. Tam kicked her sides to force her up the few stone steps, and he dragged her nose round the low grave-stones, carved with skulls and crossed bones.

At last, Meg brought him to the two arched windows in the front wall of the church. High on her saddle, Tam could see through the broken glass.

And what a sight he saw.

Chapter 3
Spying on the Locals

Tam O'Shanter saw a church full of people, all laughing and dancing, all having the wildest party he had ever seen.

But Tam didn't join them. Not yet. He just stared. Because it was also the oddest party he had ever seen.

He thought he knew some of the men and women dancing. Farmers, neighbours, old women from the woods, old men from the hills. People that he'd heard gossip about. People that he tried not to annoy, just in case his cows' milk ran dry or his family got nasty rashes and boils. All here for a midnight dance.

And what a dance. Leaping and whirling. Turning in endless circles and spirals. Going faster and higher than Tam had ever seen anyone dance before.

Tam knew some of those watching too. That was Sandy, over there. Tam had been at Sandy's funeral just last month.

Because the watchers, leaning against the walls of the church, were all cosy and snug ... in their coffins.

Their coffins were propped up against the walls. The dead bodies inside were watching the dancers with wide open sockets. Tam could see fresh corpses, dry skeletons, and all the nasty stages in between. All lighting the stony dance floor with candles held high in their bony hands, candles burning with a bright and brutal light.

Tam swallowed. Perhaps he didn't want to gate-crash this party.

He looked more closely. Why weren't those candles being blown out by the wind? Why weren't those dusty skeletons being washed clean by the rain? The church only had a few wooden roof beams left to protect it from the weather, but the floor inside was dry. The coffins were dry. The dancers weren't having to battle against the wind.

Tam twisted his neck to look up at the sky through the window. There was rain falling on his head. He could hear raindrops splashing in puddles at Meg's hooves. But there was no rain inside the church. The rain from the dark clouds above was sizzling and vanishing into steam before it fell into the church. As if the light, the music and the dancing made the air so hot that it was boiling the rain away before it could get the dancers wet.

With a shiver, Tam nudged Meg closer so that he was peeking in at the very edge of the arched window. He could still watch, but no-one inside would be able to see him. And now he was sheltered from the rain by the small bell tower above.

He looked at the dancers again. Spinning and flinging each other around to the loud music.

The music skirled and dirled even faster, even louder. Where was the music coming from? Tam leant forward to get a better view.

At the other end of the church, sitting on a wide window sill, high up on the wall, was

a huge hairy black dog

playing a massive set of red tartan bagpipes.

Tam grinned. The dog's ears flapped up and down as it pushed air into the bag. Tam almost laughed, as the dog's pink tongue licked the top of the blowpipe, and its paws struggled to hold the chanter.

Then the dog started to play a fast Scottish dance. Tam's toes started jogging and jigging along with the beat, bashing poor Meg's sides. This dog was the best piper he had ever heard.

The thunder played a drumbeat for the dog, and the lightning sent him flashing coloured lights through the cracked stained glass windows. The cold rain-drops sizzled into clouds of steam above him.

The dog was pumping air into the bag so fast and furious that the tartan cloth started to rip. The dog was gripping the wooden blowpipe so hard in its teeth that it started to splinter. But as Tam watched, the tartan wove itself back together again, and the pipe grew strong and straight again. So even though the dog broke the pipes again and again, the music never stopped.

But surely that music was much louder than one piper could play? As loud as a storm, as a crowd, as a war. The piper loud and louder blew. And the dancers quick and quicker flew.

Then Tam saw red flames in the dog's eyes, and smoke puffing from its nostrils as it blew. As the dog rocked from side to side in time with the music, and its tangled black hair flew wildly round its skull, he saw sharp little horns between its ears. At last Tam realised what he was watching.

The Devil.

In concert.

Playing live for his greatest fans.

Witches and warlocks.

Chapter 4
Too Many Bodies, Too Small a Space

Nannie wasn't nervous any more. She was having a great time at her first Friday night dance. Gossiping in the line outside, before their Master arrived, she had picked up some useful spells for sinking boats at sea and for spoiling crops on land. And already she could feel the Devil's music and power building inside her as he played.

But it was too crowded in this wee church. The kirk in Alloway was full of dead bodies and gifts, and heaving with witches from all over the country. There wasn't as much room to dance as she had hoped. Mostly she was just bouncing around in one place, her ribs jabbed by witches' elbows and her thighs bruised by warlocks' knees. But the old ones were getting tired, some of them taking a rest between the coffins. If she could stay on her feet the longest, perhaps she would get enough space to dance properly.

Then a warty old witch sat down, and Nannie had space to spin past the altar – the holy table the priests had used for their books and bits and pieces on many Sundays past. Now the table was covered in gifts the Devil's fans had brought.

There at the end, dangling down off the corner of the table, almost hidden by the other gifts, were her Granny's eyes. She laughed to think of her Granny watching her now. Dancing in the dress her Granny had made for her to wear to church.

And here she was, wearing it to church! But not as her Granny had wanted. Here she was, dancing for the Devil, dancing with all her witch's magic and all her Master's huge power. Perhaps those eyes were weeping.

But her Granny's eyes looked so small among all the other gifts. The Devil would hardly notice them. Nannie herself had to leap high to see them. She had really wanted to impress him. But other dancers had brought much bigger, better, presents:

A murderer still wrapped in the rusty chains which had held his skeleton together as his body rotted apart. He didn't have eyeballs, because the crows had picked them out, and he was missing a few toe-bones and knuckles, but most of him was still there.

Even one or two dry patches of skin still stuck to his skull and knee-caps.

And another dead criminal, this one still warm and floppy. Not a murderer but a thief. Hanged that very afternoon in Edinburgh, and brought here by the witches of Leith. Rope still tight round his neck, one last strangled breath still trapped in his gaping open mouth.

Five blunt tomahawks, axes from the Wild West, with scalped hair still stuck to their blades.

Sharp swords too, curved scimitars, still bloody to the handle from beheadings in the south.

And one knife. This wasn't a blade from battles far away, but an ordinary Scottish bread knife. Still crusty with the blood of the man it had murdered.

Three lawyers' tongues, from the courts in Glasgow, split open and turned inside out, dripping with blood and drool and lies.

And a pile of priests' hearts, from churches bigger and richer than this church had ever been, built into a black and rotting tower.

She wondered if the lawyers and priests had been alive when these gifts were removed. She wondered if they had begged for mercy, while they still had tongues to beg with, or hearts to care. And she remembered her Granny's cries last night, as Nannie plucked out her old eyes, then left her cold on the kitchen floor – Nannie's sacrifice to the Devil, so that she could have her first Friday night with the witches.

But all these gifts were bigger and from further away than her Granny's eyes. Nannie sighed. She must bring something more exciting next time. Not wet with tears, but wet with blood.

Four witches with clothes sticking to their backs and sweat dropping from their long noses and chins stopped dancing and sat down for a quick drink. Nannie grinned. They had left enough space for her to spin in a full circle.

Chapter 5
Smelly Armpits, Hairy Warts

Outside the window Tam was still sheltered from the storm against the church wall. But perhaps he should be heading home now. He'd seen enough to have a fine haunted church-yard story to tell in the pub next Friday night. He didn't need to stay any longer.

He was enjoying the music, even though he knew they were the Devil's tunes.

But he wasn't really enjoying watching a church full of old people dancing and jumping.

Old women's skirts birling round and up so that he could see their knobbly knees.

Old men kicking off their shoes so that he could see their bent toes, cracked heels and crumbling nails.

Old women twirling so fast that their long greasy grey hair slithered round their necks.

And old men panting so hard that their wrinkled faces went bright red and their warts started to glow.

Then one old woman under the window joined in a Mexican wave, and when she threw her saggy arms into the air, Tam could see and Tam could smell her sweaty hairy armpits.

He felt his Friday night beer lurch in his belly. Perhaps he should go home and have a lie down.

But just before he twitched Meg's reins to turn her away from the window and back towards the road, he saw something worth watching.

As more withered old witches sat down, he could see a tall slim girl in the middle of the church. She had shiny hair and long strong supple legs. Her dress was so short it showed her knees even when she wasn't spinning. And she hadn't been a witch long enough to have warts. Now she was starting to leap and dance. Tam smiled, and stayed to watch for a little longer.

He forgot the grim dog on the stormy pipes.

He watched the bonnie witch dance.

He forgot the warty witches in their sweaty clothes.

He watched the bonnie witch leap.

He forgot the dead bodies shaking and rattling in their coffins.

He watched the bonnie witch spin.

Chapter 6
Nannie's Solo

Now Nannie had room to feel her own power. The power she drew from the witching skills she was learning. The power she drew from the spells she was collecting. The power she drew from her first glimpse of her Master the Devil. The power she drew from his hair-raising, church-rocking, ear-splitting music.

Now she could spin so fast that the stone floor under her feet cracked and smoked.

Now she could jump so high that she could touch the last wooden rafter in the roof. Now she could dance like a witch should dance on her first ever Friday night with the Devil.

Nannie danced. The dog nodded his hairy head, and spit dripped from his wide toothy grin as he played faster, louder, higher. Nannie danced faster, the church shook, the dead waved their candles, the witches and warlocks round the walls cheered, and the thunder outside clapped.

The Devil played a final squealing note. At last there was silence. Nannie bowed, and then

a voice

from outside

called clearly:

"Well danced, bonnie lass!"

Chapter 7
Wheesht!

Tam slapped his hand over his mouth. But it was too late. They had heard him.

Suddenly the church went dark.

The dog and the pipes and the young witch and the old witches. They all vanished into the dark.

There was no sound but the wind, the rain and the thunder.

Had Tam dreamed the dance? Had he heard too many stories, and drunk too many beers, and let them mingle together in his blood to make a dream, a vision, a nightmare?

He shook his head, and started to laugh.

Of course. There hadn't been any witches. No dog. No bagpipes. No open coffins. No dancing girl. The Devil didn't visit the village of Alloway on a Friday night. What a daft idea.

Then the dark silent shell of the church erupted like a volcano. The dancers inside leapt from the hole in the top of the church, flying into the air above Tam's head, landing in the mud of the grave-yard, perching on the tops of the grave-stones. The witches shrieked and the warlocks roared and the Devil howled and they all reached for Tam.

The cracked old church bell clanged as the dancing girl leapt right through the tower, knocking the bell with her heels. She jumped down towards Tam and Meg, screeching and yelling as she fell through the rain.

And Tam screamed, all the fears of his night-time journey suddenly appearing at once. Not stories. Not dreams. Not nightmares. But real and reaching for him, right now. He screamed again.

Chapter 8
Horse Power

Tam was shaking and screaming and couldn't think what do to save himself, but Meg spun on her hooves and galloped for home.

The old grey mare left the shelter of the church and raced into the rain. She galloped past the witches and warlocks still stuck in the mud and teetering on the grave-stones. She clattered down the steps onto the road again. And Tam gripped her mane and managed to stay upright on her back.

Meg's hooves drummed on the road in time to the thunder, as the lightning ripped the sky. Tam looked back and saw the eyes and mouths of the shrieking witches behind him. Now they were pouring out through the gate, shoving and pushing each other, white warty hands and long yellow nails reaching out for him. He screamed again and kicked Meg's ribs as hard and fast as if he was sprinting on her back.

Meg turned sharp left, heading round the corner and down the hill to the bridge.

The witches and warlocks ran as fast as they could round the corner after them.

But Meg was better at running, and she galloped faster and further than they did. Galloping round the first bend on the way down the hill.

So the witches jumped and leapt into the air.

But Meg was an even better jumper, and she leapt round the second bend, towards her home, towards Tam's bed, and towards the old bridge on the way.

Then the Devil, howling and growling behind the witches, started to play his pipes, with an eerie drone and a heavy groan.

So the witches and warlocks started to dance. They danced along the curving road between the kirk and the bridge.

The witches were better at dancing than they were at running and jumping. And Meg wasn't a dancer at all, so the witches started to catch up.

The witches and warlocks danced as they had in the church, high and fast. But this time they didn't dance in circles, they danced

like a snake along the bending curving road down towards the river. A line of dancing witches turning and slithering with wicked speed closer and closer to Tam and Meg.

The Devil played faster and harder and louder, and the witches danced faster and higher and closer.

Tam heard them behind him, over the hooves and the music, over the howling and the thunder. He heard them screeching and shrieking about how they would punish him for spying on their secret dance. How they would smoke him and roast him and fry him over the Devil's fires. How they would lay his legs and arms, all sliced and ripped from his body, on their next altar, then boil him in their witches' cauldron to drink as they danced.

Then he heard a high young voice scream, "You ruined my Friday night dance!"

Meg galloped, and the Devil played, and Tam could see the old bridge over the river just a few more steps away. The deep fast running water that no evil could cross was flickering in the lightning, just out of reach.

But the Devil played even faster.

The hump-back bridge was so steep and high that Tam couldn't see to the safety on the other side. And the cobble-stones of the bridge were old and rounded and wet and slippery and Meg's speeding hooves were already sliding on the road.

Behind him the Devil played faster yet, and the girl's voice screamed even louder and much much closer. "You ruined my first Friday night!"

Clinging to Meg's back, Tam knew that safety was still very far away.

Chapter 9
Nannie or Meg

Nannie was hot and wild with anger.

Her first Friday night!

Her first dance for the Devil!

And that dripping fool of a farmer had ruined it.

He'd watched her! How dare he!

And he'd shouted out! Disturbed their dance!

He'd ruined the night for them all. But most of all for her.

Her first Friday night, and now it wouldn't be remembered for her fabulous dancing, but for that burping and babbling peeping tom.

She was so angry.

All around her, the flabby old witches and warlocks were panting and slowing. Even the vast warring music of the Devil couldn't give them enough energy to catch up with the racing grey mare.

But Nannie wasn't tired yet. It was Friday night, and she could dance all night. As the music speeded up, Nannie leapt and jumped the fastest and the furthest of all. Her long legs, her young lungs and her short skirt meant she could dance faster than any of them.

Her long white arm stretched out.

The horse's front hooves clattered on the cobble-stones of the arched bridge.

Nannie leapt for the horse as it slowed on the steep slope of the bridge. Nannie's sharpened nails reached for the man's neck. For his spine. For his heart.

But the grey horse jumped forward in one great brave bound. Almost flying, pushed onward by the loud music behind her.

And Nannie's fingers missed the man. She could only reach the horse. But suddenly the horse had leapt over the high middle stone of the bridge.

Now Nannie could go no further. Nothing evil can cross running water. She had lost her chance.

The music faded. The Devil had left them. The witches squelched off home in the rain, muttering and grumbling.

Meg trotted home, ribs heaving and eyes huge with terror. Tam slumped on her neck, his fingers clinging to her soaking wet mane, gasping his thanks, and wondering if anyone in the pub would ever believe him.

And Nannie held in her hand Meg's long grey tail, ripped from her rump, blood dripping from the end into the puddles on the road.

Nannie grinned. At least she had something a bit bigger than her Granny's eyeballs to take to the dance next Friday night.

After Friday Night ...

The very best telling of Tam's Friday night fright at Alloway Kirk is Robert Burns' poem *Tam O'Shanter*.

Robbie Burns was a famous Scottish poet, but he was also a farmer, born and brought up in the village of Alloway, and he enjoyed a drink with his mates on a Friday night (on other nights too, perhaps!). He also admitted that even though he didn't believe in them when he was thinking clearly, he still kept a sharp lookout for devils, ghosts, witches, warlocks, elf-candles, dead-lights and wraiths when he was walking alone at night.

He knew lots of old legends about the local church. One legend about a farm worker finding a boiling cauldron of arms, legs and heads hanging from the rafters. (He needed a big pot, so he poured the nasty soup out and carried it home on his head!) Another legend was about a farmer seeing a witches' dance in the church, being chased to the old bridge, and reaching safety because no evil spirits can cross the middle of a running stream.

So when Robbie Burns was asked to write a poem about the church in Alloway for a friend's book, he put all the stories he knew together to make Tam O'Shanter's tale.

Or did he? Did he make this story up from local legends and his own wonderful imagination? Or was Robbie Burns simply writing about one of his own Friday nights?

I wonder if Robert Burns had a grey horse? And I wonder how long her tail was?

BATTLE CARDS

Lari Don

Author

Favourite hero:
Hero? Heroine! I'd team up with Inanna, a Sumerian war goddess who wrestled a mountain and won.

Your weapon of choice:
Two swords. One long, one short. One in each hand. Shields are for wimps.

Favourite fight scene:
The duel on the cliff between the Man in Black and Inigo Montoya in *The Princess Bride*.

Goodie or baddie:
The baddie, definitely, but a baddie who is kind to kittens and has a really excellent swirly cloak.

RELOADED

Peter Clover

Illustrator

Favourite hero:
Wolverine from *The X-Men*!

Favourite monster:
Predator!

Your weapon of choice:
A magical sword.

Special secret power:
Speed!

Favourite fight scene:
Always the one where I win!

Goodie or baddie:
Maybe an inbetweenie! But probably a goodie!

RELOADED

Barrington Stoke would like to thank all its readers for commenting on the manuscript before publication and in particular:

Aissah
Megan Duncan
Lee Frisken
Kayleigh Geddes
Andrew Gill
Owen Grant
John Hall
Connor Higgins
Liam Jolly
Rebecca Legge
Ross Lucas
Kirsty MacIver
Moira MacIver

Mari MacKenzie
Matthew MacKenzie
Calum Mainwaring
Louise McCombie
Janet McFadden
Alysha Park
Kaysay Riddell
Kelsea Robertson
Lewis Robertson
Darias Shade
Jack Small
Neomi Smith
Rebecca Walker

Become a Consultant!

Would you like to give us feedback on our titles before they are published? Contact us at the email address below – we'd love to hear from you!

info@barringtonstoke.co.uk
www.barringtonstoke.co.uk